Disney PRINCESS

Now, thanks to the magic of Virtual 3D, you can join your favorite princesses in amazing animations on your computer screen.

Virtual 3D is easy! Here's what you have to do . . .

1

Check that your computer has a webcam, and that it can run the Virtual 3D software (see the minimum system requirements panel on the previous page).

2

Next, go online to the website www.parragon.com/bookscomealive to download the V3D software. Follow the on-screen instructions to install the software on your computer and then start the program!

3

As you go through the book, look for special V3D panels that will tell you which interactive animation card to use. While the software is running, hold each interactive animation card in front of your webcam to begin the fun!

Four amazing Virtual 3D experiences!

Dress for the ball with Cinderella

Dance with Belle in the ballroom

Help Ariel collect underwater treasures

...ers in ...unzel's hair

PICTURE CREDITS
© 2013 Disney Enterprises, Inc

TEXT AND DESIGN BY CARLTON BOOKS
WRITER: Emily Stead
EXECUTIVE EDITOR: Selina Wood
ART EDITOR: Emily Clarke
AUGMENTED REALITY COORDINATORS: Jake Da'Costa, Tracy Tsang
CREATIVE DIRECTOR: Clare Baggaley
PRODUCTION: Christine Ni

This edition published by Parragon in 2013
Parragon
Chartist House
15–17 Trim Street
Bath BA1 1HA, UK
www.parragon.com

Copyright © 2013 Disney Enterprises, Inc.

ISBN 978-1-4723-0537-4

Printed in China

A Virtual 3D Book

Cinderella

Selfless Cinderella never stops believing she will find true happiness one day, even when her mean stepmother makes her work as a servant in her own home. Cinderella's dreams come true with the wave of a wand from the Fairy Godmother who grants her greatest wish—to go to the royal ball!

"A dream is a wish your heart makes."

VIRTUAL 3D

See the Fairy Godmother appear in a sparkle of fairy dust, as if by magic! Then let her get you all dressed up for the ball.

Princess Profile

Character: Cinderella is kind, gentle, and cheerful.

Her name means: "Cinderella" comes from the word "cinders," which means ashes. One of her jobs was to tend the fire.

Favorite outfit: A beautiful blue ball gown that matches her eyes.

Friends: Mice Gus and Jaq . . . and the Fairy Godmother!

Villains: Lady Tremaine and her daughters Anastasia and Drizella.

True Love

Prince Charming is true to his name. A handsome prince and gentleman, the Prince falls in love with Cinderella the moment he sets eyes on her at the ball.

Cinderella's animal friends always have time for their "Cinderelly" and give her a helping hand whenever they can.

Secret Fact:
The first pink dress that Cinderella tried on for the ball belonged to her mother.

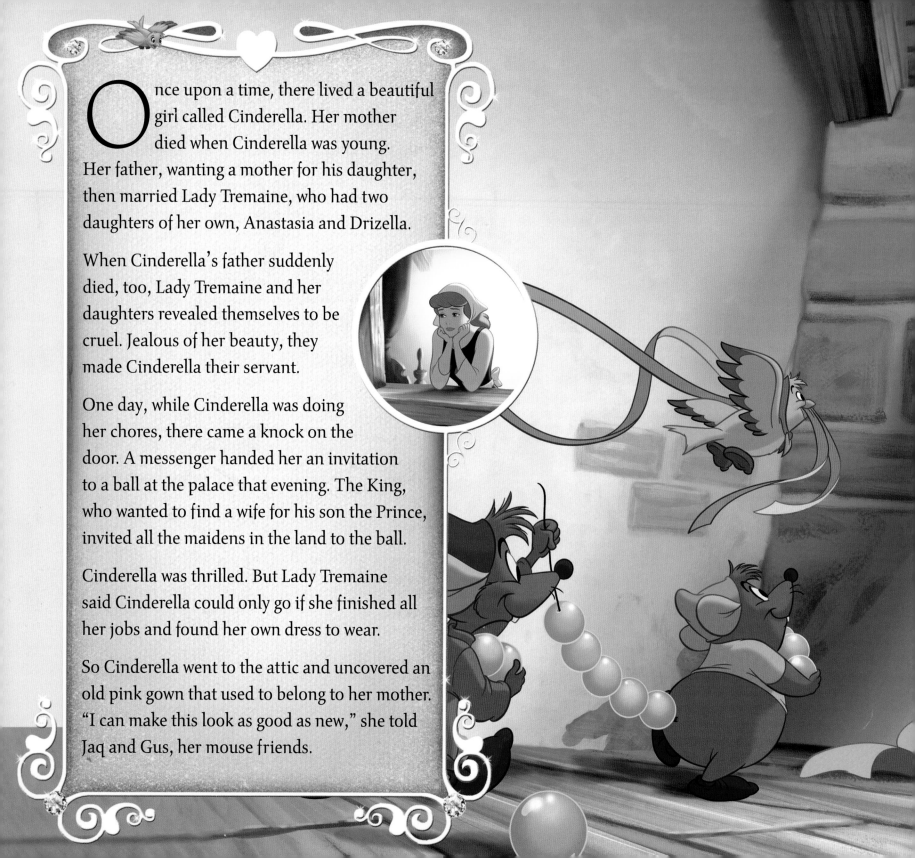

Once upon a time, there lived a beautiful girl called Cinderella. Her mother died when Cinderella was young. Her father, wanting a mother for his daughter, then married Lady Tremaine, who had two daughters of her own, Anastasia and Drizella.

When Cinderella's father suddenly died, too, Lady Tremaine and her daughters revealed themselves to be cruel. Jealous of her beauty, they made Cinderella their servant.

One day, while Cinderella was doing her chores, there came a knock on the door. A messenger handed her an invitation to a ball at the palace that evening. The King, who wanted to find a wife for his son the Prince, invited all the maidens in the land to the ball.

Cinderella was thrilled. But Lady Tremaine said Cinderella could only go if she finished all her jobs and found her own dress to wear.

So Cinderella went to the attic and uncovered an old pink gown that used to belong to her mother. "I can make this look as good as new," she told Jaq and Gus, her mouse friends.

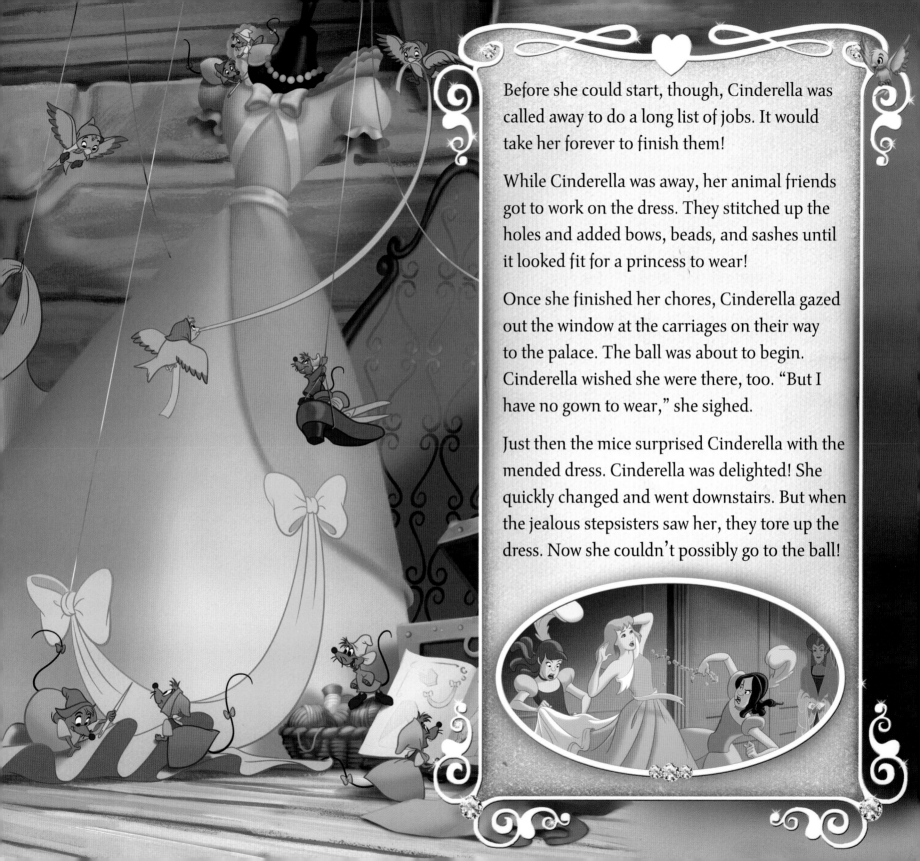

Before she could start, though, Cinderella was called away to do a long list of jobs. It would take her forever to finish them!

While Cinderella was away, her animal friends got to work on the dress. They stitched up the holes and added bows, beads, and sashes until it looked fit for a princess to wear!

Once she finished her chores, Cinderella gazed out the window at the carriages on their way to the palace. The ball was about to begin. Cinderella wished she were there, too. "But I have no gown to wear," she sighed.

Just then the mice surprised Cinderella with the mended dress. Cinderella was delighted! She quickly changed and went downstairs. But when the jealous stepsisters saw her, they tore up the dress. Now she couldn't possibly go to the ball!

Upset, Cinderella went walking in the woods, where she met the Fairy Godmother. "You shall go to the ball!" exclaimed the Fairy Godmother and waved her wand. Before Cinderella's eyes, a pumpkin turned into a glittering carriage, and the mice became horses!

Next, the Fairy Godmother pointed her wand at Cinderella. With a "Bibbidi-Bobbidi-Boo!" Cinderella was wearing a beautiful blue ball gown and a pair of sparkling glass slippers.

Right when it was Anastasia and Drizella's turn to dance with the Prince, Cinderella arrived at the ball. She was the most beautiful girl the Prince had ever seen, and he went straight to ask her to dance. The Prince and Cinderella took a stroll in the moonlight. The couple were falling in love. But the clock was about to strike midnight!

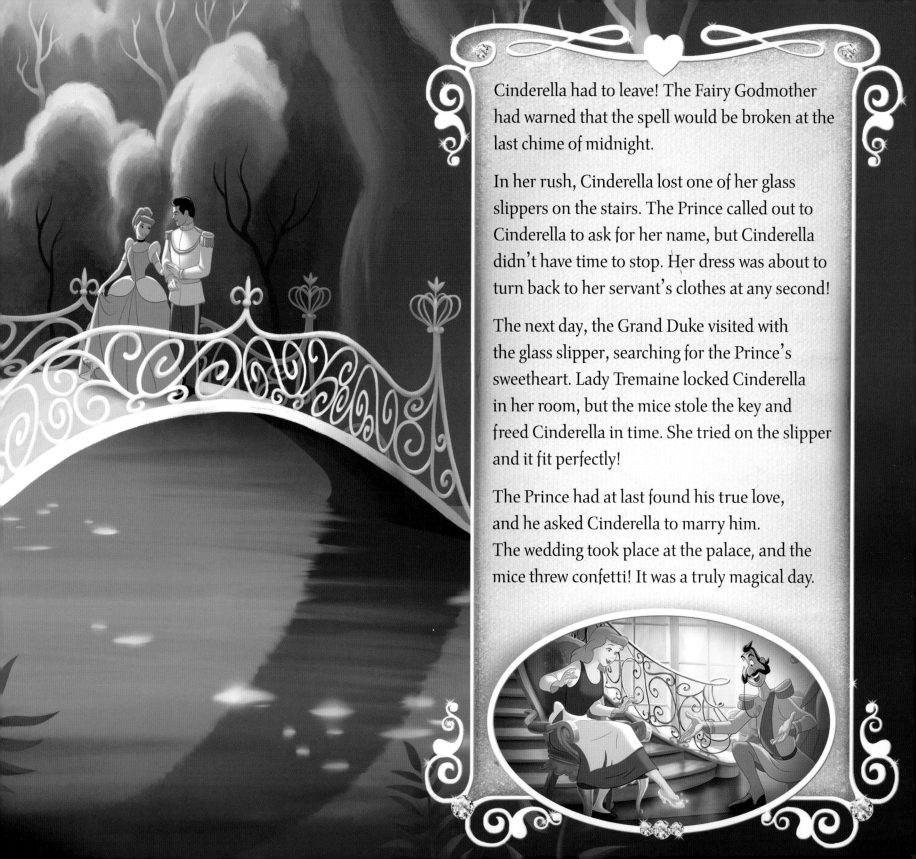

Cinderella had to leave! The Fairy Godmother had warned that the spell would be broken at the last chime of midnight.

In her rush, Cinderella lost one of her glass slippers on the stairs. The Prince called out to Cinderella to ask for her name, but Cinderella didn't have time to stop. Her dress was about to turn back to her servant's clothes at any second!

The next day, the Grand Duke visited with the glass slipper, searching for the Prince's sweetheart. Lady Tremaine locked Cinderella in her room, but the mice stole the key and freed Cinderella in time. She tried on the slipper and it fit perfectly!

The Prince had at last found his true love, and he asked Cinderella to marry him. The wedding took place at the palace, and the mice threw confetti! It was a truly magical day.

Belle

It is no surprise that Gaston, the most handsome man in the village, wants to marry beautiful Belle. But Belle is more interested in the faraway places she reads about in her books, and could never marry shallow Gaston. She is searching for someone special who will share her dreams.

VIRTUAL 3D

Hold your Belle card in your hand and wave at her. Then see her dance the waltz with the Beast!

Princess Profile

Character: Belle is smart, brave, curious, and loves books.

Her name means: Belle is the word for "beautiful" in French.

Favorite outfit: A fabulous yellow dress with matching gloves.

Family: Her father, Maurice, is an inventor.

Friends: Lumiere, Mrs. Potts, Chip, and Cogsworth.

Villain: Gaston

True Love

Although it is not love at first sight, at least not for Belle, a genuine love between Belle and the Beast blossoms as they spend more time together. Beneath his fierce exterior, the Beast has a kind heart.

Belle always has her head in a book. She wants to learn about the world around her.

Secret Fact:
When Belle goes home to see her father, Chip secretly travels with her!

Once upon a time, there lived a beautiful young woman named Belle. She loved to read more than anything else in the world, and dreamed of visiting the faraway places mentioned in her books.

There was a hunter who lived nearby called Gaston. He believed he was the most handsome man in the town, and wished to marry Belle. Belle, though, did not return his affection. She could never love such a selfish man.

Belle lived with her father, Maurice, an inventor. The townspeople thought that Maurice was foolish, but Belle always had faith in him. One day, when Belle's father was taking his inventions to a fair, he got lost in the dark woods. When his horse ran away, Maurice stumbled upon the gates to an enchanted castle.

Once inside, Maurice discovered that some of the things in the household could talk! He met a teapot, Mrs. Potts, and her son Chip, a funny candelabra named Lumiere, and a clock, Cogsworth.

But they were not alone in the castle —it belonged to a terrifying beast, who locked Maurice in a dark dungeon!

The Beast had once been a handsome and selfish prince. Then one day, an old woman had come to the castle seeking shelter. When the Prince had refused to let her in, the woman had revealed herself as an enchantress, and turned the Prince into a fearsome beast to teach him a lesson!

The spell could only be broken if the Beast fell in love, and if he was loved in return.

When Belle learned that her father was missing, she set off to search for him. Maurice's horse led her through the woods to the castle.

She found her father in the dungeon, but soon came face to face with the enormous Beast. At first she was scared, but Belle pleaded bravely with the Beast to release her father and take her prisoner instead. The Beast agreed, but made Belle promise that she would remain at the castle forever.

Maurice rushed back to the town to get help to rescue Belle, but no one believed his story about the terrifying beast in the castle.

As time passed, Belle grew to care for the Beast. She realized that she had nothing to fear from him. Instead, the Beast turned out to be kind and gentle. And as for the Beast, before long, he found that he had fallen in love with Belle.

One night, the pair shared a special dinner together. Belle wore an elegant yellow gown. She had never looked more beautiful. Lumiere and the others hoped that Belle and the Beast would declare their love for each other, so that the enchantress' spell would be broken.

After dinner, they went to the ballroom and waltzed by candlelight. Although it was a magical evening, the Beast knew that Belle missed her father. He let Belle see her father in an enchanted mirror. When Belle saw Maurice lost and alone, the Beast, in a noble act, allowed her to leave and go to his aid.

Before long, Belle arrived back in town. Gaston greeted her and asked her to marry him, but Belle refused. Out of spite, he called for her father to be sent to an asylum. Belle showed the townspeople a picture of the Beast in the enchanted mirror, to try to prove that her father had been telling the truth.

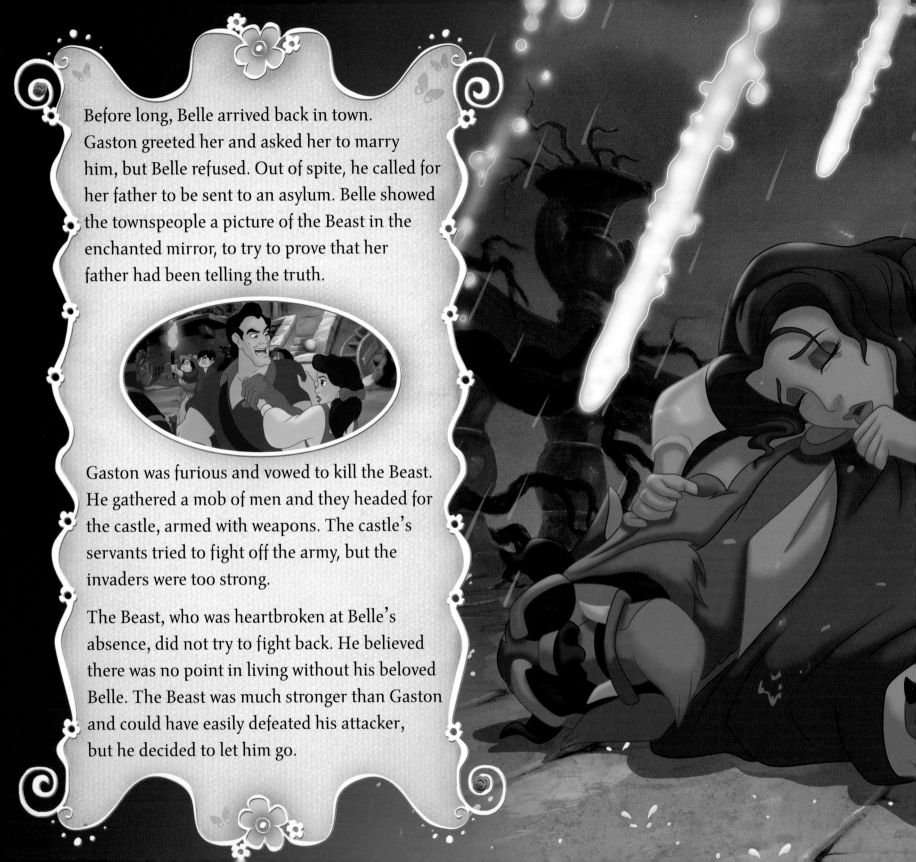

Gaston was furious and vowed to kill the Beast. He gathered a mob of men and they headed for the castle, armed with weapons. The castle's servants tried to fight off the army, but the invaders were too strong.

The Beast, who was heartbroken at Belle's absence, did not try to fight back. He believed there was no point in living without his beloved Belle. The Beast was much stronger than Gaston and could have easily defeated his attacker, but he decided to let him go.

Belle returned to the castle, desperate to warn the Beast. When Belle arrived, the Beast climbed up to a balcony to meet her. But as he did so, Gaston crept up behind the Beast and plunged a sword into his back.

With tears in her eyes, Belle leaned over the Beast's body. "I love you," she whispered, as he lay dying. Instantly, something magical happened. The Beast's body rose into the air and returned to its human form!

The spell was broken, and the Beast was a handsome prince once again! He took Belle in his arms and she realized that standing there, before her eyes, was her beloved Beast.

In the castle, Mrs. Potts, Chip, Cogsworth, and Lumiere changed back to humans, too. The next day, a delighted crowd gathered to watch Belle and her prince perform a waltz in the ballroom. Everyone agreed it was true love and, of course, Belle and the Prince lived happily ever after.

Ariel

"Watch and you'll see —someday I'll be part of your world."

Meet Ariel, a mermaid who dreams of one day becoming human and having adventures above the waves. She will do anything to try to make her dreams come true. Trouble is never far away from this princess of the sea, but luckily, Ariel's friends and family are always there to help.

VIRTUAL 3D

Enter Ariel's magical underwater world! Help her collect trinkets for her treasure collection. Then Sebastian has a treat for you!

Princess Profile

Character: Ariel is curious, adventurous, and a little stubborn.

Likes: Adventures, writing music.

Favorite outfit: A shimmering purple dress given to her by her father.

Family: She is the youngest of King Triton's seven daughters.

Friends: Flounder, Sebastian, and Scuttle.

Villain: Ursula is a cruel enchantress.

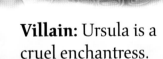

True Love

Prince Eric is a gallant sailor, and he's determined to meet the girl who saved his life. Eric and Ariel are perfect for each other because they both love life at sea! Bravery is one of Eric's greatest qualities, which he shows when he defeats Ursula to save Ariel and King Triton.

Ariel loves collecting things from the human world. She hides these treasures in a secret cavern.

Secret Fact:
Sebastian the crab's full name is Horatio Thelonius Ignatius Crustatious Sebastian!

Once upon a time, in an underwater kingdom called Atlantica, there lived a little mermaid called Ariel. She was curious about the world above the sea and wished more than anything else to be human.

One day, she swam up and looked over the side of a ship and saw a handsome man, Prince Eric. Suddenly, a storm broke out and a bolt of lightning struck the ship. Eric was washed overboard. Ariel pulled him onto dry land and sang a beautiful melody to him.

As Eric's eyes began to open, Ariel heard people approaching, and she quickly splashed below the waves. Eric decided he must find the girl who had saved his life. Although he hadn't seen her, he felt sure he'd recognize her voice if he heard it again.

When Ariel's father, King Triton, discovered that Ariel had been spending time near humans, he was furious. "You know that contact with humans is forbidden!" he roared at his daughter.

Ariel was heartbroken. Then two eels named Flotsam and Jetsam approached her. They belonged to the wicked sea witch, Ursula. They promised that their mistress could make Ariel's dreams come true.

In exchange for Ariel's voice, Ursula offered to give Ariel legs so that she could walk on land with Eric. Ariel had three days during which she must make Eric fall in love with her. If Eric kissed her, Ariel would be allowed to stay human forever. If he didn't, then Ariel would belong to Ursula forever!

Ariel signed a contract, agreeing to the deal. Ursula took Ariel's voice and kept it in a shell, tied around her neck.

Right away, Ariel found herself transformed into a human. She walked along the beach in delight and, all of a sudden, she met Prince Eric.

Without her voice, Ariel couldn't speak—or sing—but Eric had a feeling that this was the same girl who had rescued him. The pair took a boat ride together and almost kissed, but Flotsam and Jetsam overturned the boat!

When Ursula found out, she disguised herself as a pretty woman called Vanessa. She began to sing, using Ariel's voice, and Prince Eric was instantly enchanted. Under her spell, Eric believed that Vanessa was his true love and asked her to be his wife. They would marry at sunset on a ship.

But Ariel's loyal friend, Scuttle the seagull, saw Vanessa through one of the ship's portholes. She was looking in a mirror, but the reflection staring back at her belonged to Ursula!

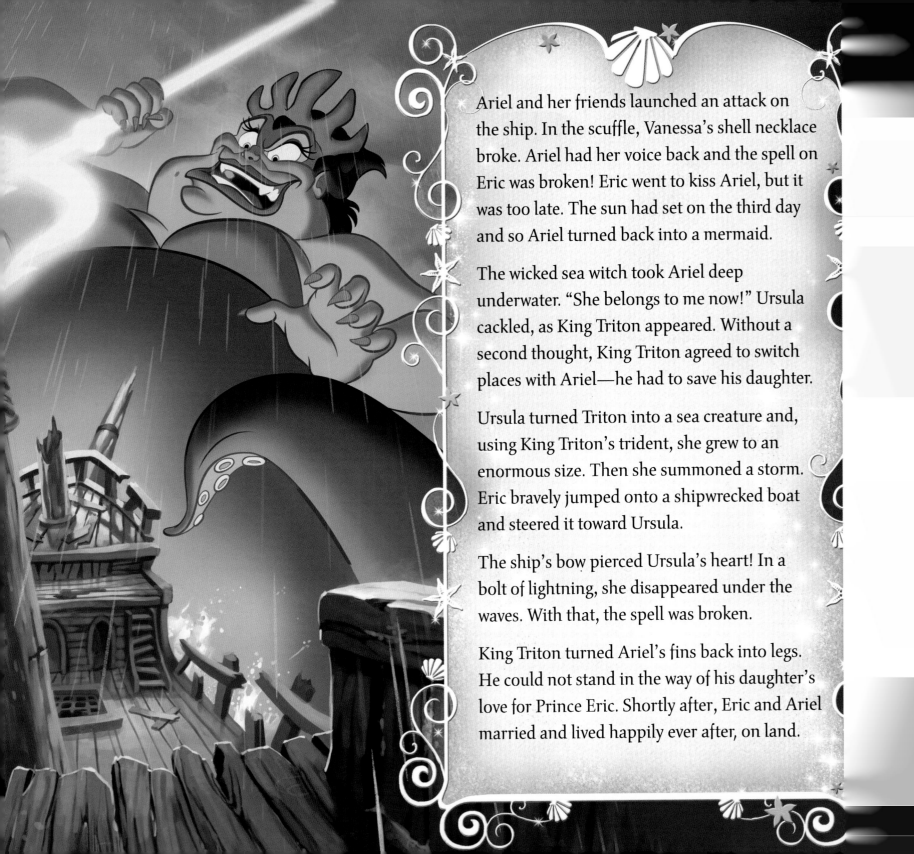

Ariel and her friends launched an attack on the ship. In the scuffle, Vanessa's shell necklace broke. Ariel had her voice back and the spell on Eric was broken! Eric went to kiss Ariel, but it was too late. The sun had set on the third day and so Ariel turned back into a mermaid.

The wicked sea witch took Ariel deep underwater. "She belongs to me now!" Ursula cackled, as King Triton appeared. Without a second thought, King Triton agreed to switch places with Ariel—he had to save his daughter.

Ursula turned Triton into a sea creature and, using King Triton's trident, she grew to an enormous size. Then she summoned a storm. Eric bravely jumped onto a shipwrecked boat and steered it toward Ursula.

The ship's bow pierced Ursula's heart! In a bolt of lightning, she disappeared under the waves. With that, the spell was broken.

King Triton turned Ariel's fins back into legs. He could not stand in the way of his daughter's love for Prince Eric. Shortly after, Eric and Ariel married and lived happily ever after, on land.

Rapunzel

Rapunzel is the girl with the golden locks who was stolen away from her parents as a baby. Imprisoned in a tower by the evil Mother Gothel, Rapunzel longs to get a closer look at the floating lanterns that appear on her birthday each year. Rapunzel's life changes forever when a thief climbs the tower one day . . . .

"Now's when my life begins!"

VIRTUAL 3D

Decorate Rapunzel's hair with beautiful flowers, then watch in wonder as the floating lanterns appear!

Princess Profile

Character: Rapunzel is feisty, energetic, spirited, and courageous.

Family: The King and Queen (her father and mother).

Favorite outfit: A purple skirt with a lavender corset, though Rapunzel would look pretty in whatever she wore.

Friends: Flynn Rider, Pascal the chameleon, and Maximus the horse.

Villain: Mother Gothel is not to be trusted.

True Love

Flynn Rider grew up in an orphanage. Flynn is not his real name—he changed it as he wanted to be like the hero from his favorite book. Rapunzel is glad she is able to meet the real Eugene Fitzherbert, who is brave and trustworthy.

Even though she is stuck in the tower, Rapunzel stays busy painting, knitting, and playing the guitar.

Secret Fact:
Rapunzel's amazing blond hair is 70 feet long —that's longer than two buses put together!

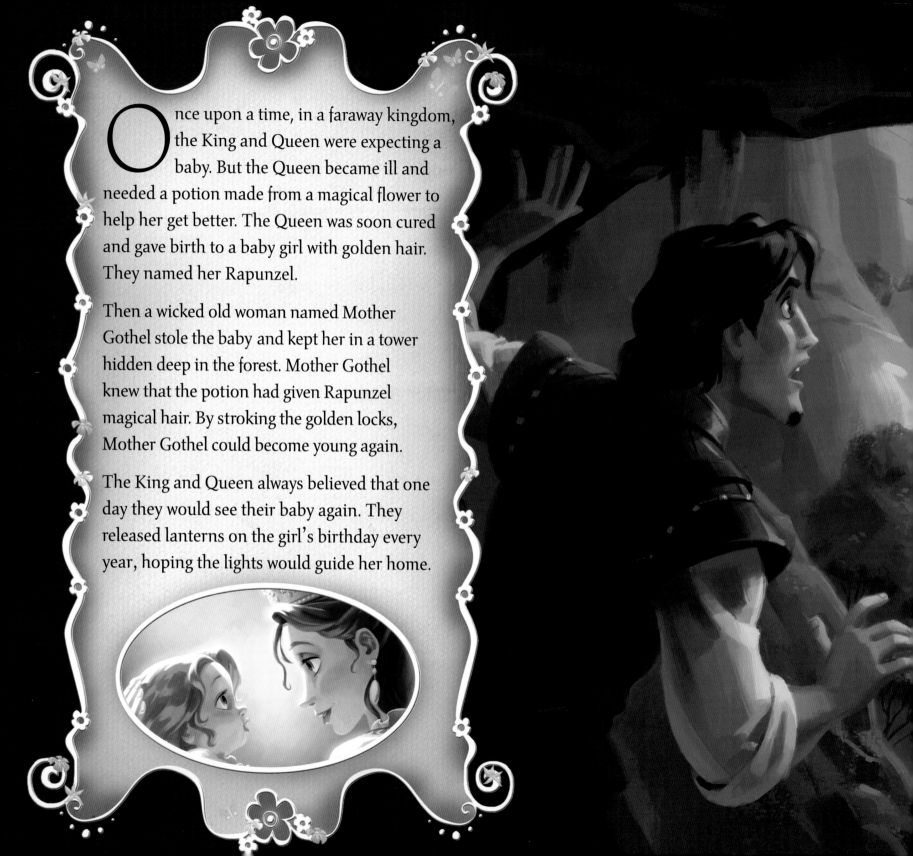

Once upon a time, in a faraway kingdom, the King and Queen were expecting a baby. But the Queen became ill and needed a potion made from a magical flower to help her get better. The Queen was soon cured and gave birth to a baby girl with golden hair. They named her Rapunzel.

Then a wicked old woman named Mother Gothel stole the baby and kept her in a tower hidden deep in the forest. Mother Gothel knew that the potion had given Rapunzel magical hair. By stroking the golden locks, Mother Gothel could become young again.

The King and Queen always believed that one day they would see their baby again. They released lanterns on the girl's birthday every year, hoping the lights would guide her home.

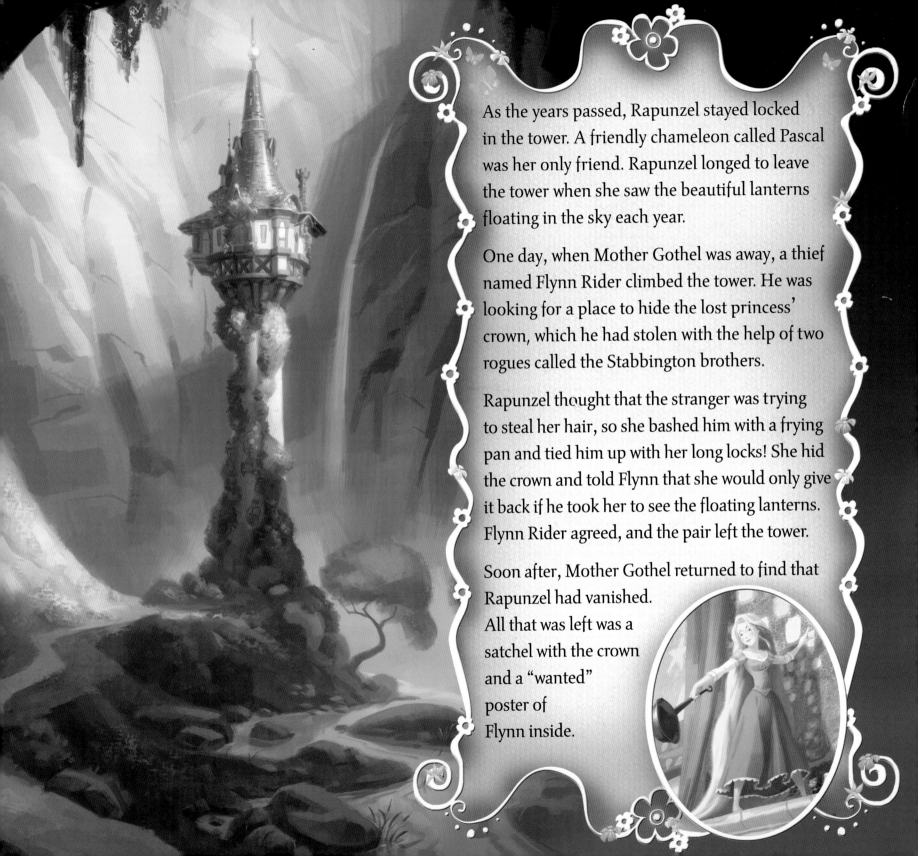

As the years passed, Rapunzel stayed locked in the tower. A friendly chameleon called Pascal was her only friend. Rapunzel longed to leave the tower when she saw the beautiful lanterns floating in the sky each year.

One day, when Mother Gothel was away, a thief named Flynn Rider climbed the tower. He was looking for a place to hide the lost princess' crown, which he had stolen with the help of two rogues called the Stabbington brothers.

Rapunzel thought that the stranger was trying to steal her hair, so she bashed him with a frying pan and tied him up with her long locks! She hid the crown and told Flynn that she would only give it back if he took her to see the floating lanterns. Flynn Rider agreed, and the pair left the tower.

Soon after, Mother Gothel returned to find that Rapunzel had vanished. All that was left was a satchel with the crown and a "wanted" poster of Flynn inside.